Praise for Diane Williams

"An operation worthy of a master spy, a double agent in the house of fiction. . . . Diane Williams conjures up an edgy, jagged state of mind, a lurching consciousness in a culture of speed and amnesia."
—Matthew Stadler, *New York Times*

"These stories will drive you crazy in the way readers of serious fiction need to be driven out of their heads occasionally."—*Chicago Sun-Times*

"The mood is never less than edgy, and it sometimes rises to real horror. . . . These fictional chips glitter with a shiny, irreducible strangeness that wills us to think twice."—Elizabeth Tallent, *Los Angeles Times*

"Diane Williams dares you to keep up with her—an admirable attitude in fiction."—Amy Hempel

"Williams tears into the worlds of love, death, outlaw sexuality and the strange workings of society with a ferocity that is rather rare. . . . These stories should be read not only as challenges to traditional aesthetic sensibilities, but also as ways to refigure our own lives."—*Pittsburgh Press*

"Williams offers up pagefuls of brilliant, often blackly comic, epiphanies and deep glances into those intervals between perceptions, when doubt can send hairline fractures through the stoutest point of view."
—Eli Gottlieb, *Elle*

"Like Donald Barthelme and Franz Kafka, Williams at times is able to boil down the obtuse complexities of the body, the mind, the soul, etc., and fashion them into a compact cudgel with the power to flatten the receptive reader."
—*Dallas Morning News*

"Williams's miniatures cast long shadows, while offering unexpected meanings to the light which edges them."—Bradford Morrow

ROMANCER ERECTOR

ROMANCER ERECTOR

Novella and Stories

DIANE WILLIAMS

Dalkey Archive Press

Library of Congress Cataloging-in-Publication Data:

Williams, Diane
Romancer erector / Diane Williams.— 1st ed.
p. cm.
ISBN 1-56478-312-X (alk. paper)
1. Experimental fiction, American.   I. Title.
PS3573.I44846 R6 2001
813'.54—dc21
2001028787

Acknowledgment is made to the following publications in which these stories
first appeared, some in different versions and sometimes under different titles.

*Alaska Quarterly Review, American Letters & Commentary, Black Book,
Boston Review, Cimarron Review, Colorado Review, Conjunctions,
CrossConnect: Writers of the Information Age, Denver Quarterly, Dominion
Review, Elimae, Epoch, 5 Trope, Gargoyle, Impossible Object, The Iowa
Review, The Ohio Review, The Pushcart Prize 2000 XXIV, Salt Hill, Web Del Sol*

Partially funded by a grant from the Illinois Arts Council, a state agency.

Dalkey Archive Press books are published by the
Center for Book Culture, a nonprofit organization with
offices in Chicago and Normal, Illinois.

www.dalkeyarchive.com

I must eat my dinner.

—WILLIAM SHAKESPEARE

CONTENTS

Nancy Weak

1

Can't one be less sorrowful?

"Look! she upsets me," Aborn said. "We ought to be able to enjoy ourselves without worrying about her one way or the other."

She stepped over a stone, a stone, not exactly. At the very least, what began as loitering in the green yard, was not calming for her.

She wore the sundress which was not dull enough and with every stride she took, her hair was bumped by her hat.

2

She entered an old-fashioned shop on a famous street where more than several damaged objects are kept.

"Can I help you?" an old-fashioned woman said.

"Oh, you have this!" Nancy said. "It isn't comfortable. It hurts. It's heavy."

"Yes. It picks up all of the lights in the evening."

"I have never seen anything like this!" Nancy said.

Then as a household fly might do rudely, Nancy left the shop in a rush.

3

In this same year Aborn stumped toward Nancy.

He was intending to be useful to her, not to appear to be ill-timed or unreasonable. If he gave her hand a friendly shake, he might startle her.

Even so, she was roughly grasped from behind.

Unaware who held her, she tried to pull free.

She thought, I may be in distress!

She worked to free herself, did not turn, did not speak.

The scent of the assailant surrounded her.

Presently, she was let go.

"Mr. Aborn!" Nancy said.

"Nancy!" he said, "I wish I could think of your last name."

4

"Oh, my God! My name is Nancy! You saw me."

No, no, no doubt, Aborn saw all of her displeasure, how unsafe she was.

"My dear!" he said, "I like your hat!"

"Thanks," she said. "I got right into bed and went to sleep after you left."

"Then you must have felt fine."

"I don't understand," is what she said.

Past the terrified shrubs, they bothered to go, and then they went along toward an old-fashioned shop where Nancy pressed the bell. When the bell signalled its habitual reaction, they went on in.

5

"That's what I want," said Nancy.

"Did you look at everything they have?" Aborn said. "Let us look at everything."

"This is eighteen years old," she said. "That's old-fashioned. Is it old-fashioned enough for you?"

"Which one do you want?" Aborn said.

"Is that old enough? This one," Nancy said, "is sweet."

6

She chose the brooch-mounted badge.

Well, well, next they sat side by side in a taxicab sedan. They had joined in a certain stylistic grace when Nancy pressed her lips together and pinched her baize.

The world was high, large, long, crammed.

At the restaurant things are not too bad.

There's a pancake for dessert.

The server's face—her hopeful fur-lined eyes—please Nancy.

Nancy wants to charm this girl. She is unable to resist that, so the server says slyly, "I am going to forget you," when the moment for parting is clear.

7

It was a breezy lightness they ambled into. Many things were being put upon. A huge flowery bush had no self-command.

Nancy's petals bulged a bit. She had bought herself some roses. She was not horribly sleepy and the dream flowers, the unpretentious hovels, and the places all about were particularly advanced in years.

Aborn, quite brightly, went on ahead, all by himself, in search of some dandy souls he'd never known
before.

Where are you now? Nancy had to think at the
interior of her house, as she unwrapped her buds
and trimmed their eensy stems with the boning knife.

The roses were just too weary and they fell all
over themselves.

Still, she did encourage them so that they did not
lose heart inside of their tankard, nor did they ever
much resemble the living things.

9

Her immature new brooch she skewered onto herself, and she hung her hat on the genitalia of a chair.

The roses were okay. They were scented with
Beconase.

10

Those Floradora roses.

"Hi," said the girl to her old mother who was
dressed in quilted slippers and bunchy clothes.

"Good afternoon," the woman said, "dear."

11

Nancy's father would have to fuck the old woman when he got home, so the old guy fucked her.

Hush!—they went up the stairs to do this in a room pale as this is where among other things the tables are surmounted by lamps and the decorations are bronze-tinted.

Welcome to the afternoon.

With slight astonishment, both the mother and the father understand they're happy.

"I will, of course, I will, if you want me to, do it again," the old man told her.

"No, dear, you rest," his old wife said.

12

Nancy's old mother is so old. She is such an outmoded thing, even the finger ring she wears is a mess.

It should be kept on her body for the best results.

13

Nancy's father is ordinarily weak.

"Can you remember?" his wife says to him, "something good about me? Would you remind me?"

Now when she comes to her senses again, her

inclination to be angry often creeps across a plate and folds back its wings.

Her husband collects his thoughts, some adornments and his shoes.

"Sit by me," this mother of a few incongruous people says.

She sits in the expectant chair. One of her feet is curled on its side, all floaty on the floor.

Her mouth aches. Her irradiated eyes are fine.

She is regarded in certain circles as a slacker.

14

"The floors look bad," the old man says. "Next time bleach them or use a more powerful cleaner."

"No," she says, "I'll bleach them."

15

The husband's favorite thing is even nicer than I am.

16

When the mother is interrupted by one of her wishes, she mashes it. She says, "Tell me again how did Len die?"

17

"He was an independent boy," his father said.
"How did he die?" the mother asks.
"He was killed," said Nancy.
"Not entirely," said the father.
The old woman said, "He was not killed."
"No," said the father, "as I said before, his head, his head was lopped off with a clasp-knife." Whatever that is.

18

Father, oh father of people!
"I hurt my head," he said, rubbing a knob on his face near his odd ear.
His old wife is not as well-liked any more.

19

And the old man, who for an instant appears highly intellectual, shows his wife his scrotum.
She says, "Well."

20

He could see the sharp small hairs on the old wife's arm and above her mouth.

21

During the intermission, Aborn arrives.

"Just point the way," said Nancy. "Thank you."

Aborn had stepped out from somewhere.

22

The old woman butchers bread to a fare-thee-well.

Upstairs the topsheets won't overstrain themselves. Nancy puts her hand down on some intelligent native surface when she does not wear her loose outer garment or her overshoes with the thick wooden soles. She is lying down and the original extent of her relief points upward undoubtably.

Very, Very Red

I have too much of a sense of myself as a man to be reckless. I tell myself, "Get it done!" Robert and Buster have volunteered to help me, but I am not an invalid, Mary.

I have asked myself this question: "What does she need?"

Mary, I am not ashamed she is naked in the bed, waiting for me. I told her I knew how to behave. This time, however, when I became bored, I had a very, very, very, very long conversation with Diane, Mary.

She says, "Remember who you are. Remember what you do." She promises me that I will be pleasantly surprised. She promises. Sometimes, afterward, I hate her. She pities me.

You poor thing is what she says.

I will yawn significantly after dinner. "Diane," I will say, "isn't it time that we went up to bed?" Mary, you say to ask Diane to give me one of her fancy handjobs. Will you be home on Saturday?

I thanked Diane for petting me.

These days Diane's skin is waxy, cold. She fell off of the chesterfield. She was weary from swimming. I did not try to help her. I was afraid, so this is sad. I unfastened her belt. My hand was strong enough, capable enough. I remember. I remember my enjoyment of our happy home.

We went into the dining room, and Gretch came over to us and Gretch said, "You can have whatever you want!"

Gretch is another one. I am going to sleep with Diane and I am going to sleep with Bill's wife.

Buster said he didn't like Diane as much as he liked our other girlfriend.

"Better eat up those peaches," Buster said.

I said, "Buster, right."

Buster, Buster, Buster.

Perhaps, Mary, I just want to see what will happen to Buster.

One would not know why any of this is, if this is a drama or if this is a pageant.

Mary?—could you be with me here, Mary? This would not make things easier for me. I just wanted somebody like you to change her mind.

I don't have to say everything I could say about Diane.

The doctor asked Buster to carry Diane in. Her skirt was short. She had bobbed her hair.

She accepted a cigarette from Buster once she was back up on the chesterfield. She also accepted an ashtray from Buster, and she did a lot of throat-clearing. The doctor treated her like a friend. "Do you have a sore throat?" the doctor asked her.

She'd be perfectly capable of that. I think Diane did have a sore throat! Diane is lifelike.

"I'll have a cup of tea!" Diane said.

They all agreed with her about that.

"She can always make me laugh," Mother said. "She is the smartest person I know!"

I will tell you this—I had the shivers and my neck hurt from sitting in my chair. "I love you with all of my heart," I told Diane. I think it is thrilling to hear people say that.

Diane said she would not mind if I told you how she and I do it—I am on top of her, then a little on the side of her.

What a night! I thought I saw you and somebody else, high up on our wall, tiny-sized, getting ready to fuck each other, or you were just finishing up. Together, we had here great rivals in a house.

There are many imitations of Diane here, made of horn and rubber and plastic.

I merely tapped Harriet and she broke.

I wonder what this is. Diane was wearing crazy clothes. Her hat fell off of the chesterfield where she had set it.

She had sprung back into a curled position. We washed the girl carefully.

You think to yourself, I slept with that thing.

What Diane still needs is what I need. She said that after the party she had sobbed and sobbed and sobbed. I have heard her tell that story before.

I gave a little tap tap to the vagina of Diane—where there was a sizable stain on it—ink—still wet. I thought she would go around like this.

It was so easy when I took Diane to the bed. "Isn't this a nice ruffle?" I said.

For your information I said, "What did they do to you Diane? Did they sew you up? Look how little you have made it!"

Aren't I a lucky boy?

Diane gave me something which looks like Honorene. Diane fixed it so that I could wear it on my little finger. It's a little chipped. It's a little uncomfortable. It's tight on me.

Diane said, "I think I got that in Burma."

When Diane asked me for it, I threw it across the room. Just joking.

I had expected I would be sympathetic to Diane.

I woke up sexy and frightened, thinking about the girls in the window stacked up on top of each other, and thinking about you, you frightening person.

I have been expecting a nice compliment from you.

When Buster tried to protect Diane, they threw Buster across the room.

They pointed at Diane, and Buster tried to protect Diane. They threw Buster across the room.

Diane had her hat on and Diane said, "Where are we going?" and I said, "What do you mean where are we going?" and Diane said, "I am going with you."

I said, "Oh, Diane! Diane, oh, no!"

One day she just left town and she went out West. She called me, she said, "I won the lottery."

Diane—the girl—she was not running away from me! I did a dumb thing! I did such a dumb thing! My hair is sticking out of my head because I did such a dumb thing!

Buster returned here with Diane, saying that he had not had much fun with her. He carried Diane back to the hiding place after we had eaten our dinner with Betty.

Diane's vulva is a bit better now. She wears lip rouge. She wears a necklace of pearls. She wiped her hands.

She can climb in, she can climb out of an automobile. She can drive an automobile up onto, up on top of a roadway. She will do the cutest little trick. We are going to have to touch her vulva.

We were not wrong in believing that she had been

a full-fledged girl at one point. We thought of touching the vulva.

We have pried her apart, divided her again, discarded the center portion, given her a good soaking. We behave, for what it is worth, with our dicks protruding, as if we were gentlemen.

I have worked pretty hard at this. This has taken me a long time. I expected this to be scratched or chipped by now. I am surprised it isn't.

Diane touched the collar bar you gave me. People must think it is a sin for me to wear this.

She said, "What is this?"

I said, "I found it. Somebody gave it to me. I found it."

She said, "Which? Did you find it? Or did somebody give it to you?"

I said, "Both!"

Now you listen, I do not do anything too strenuous. People say I did not leave the garden. That is not true. This is a lie.

My clothing was described. Only what a woman wears is this interesting.

Mary, I spoke to Diane as frankly as I speak to you. I thought Diane was doing fine. There was a fluttering. I felt a tickling. I was stung.

I said, "I was stung." I said, "Would you look, Diane?" I said, "Diane, dear, Olga wouldn't mind it if you fished around inside of my trousers."

"Diane, you have been here forever," Olga said,

"haven't you?"

"No," Diane said, "just for two years."

A woman asked us if we had seen Diane. The woman said, "That one wasn't Diane."

I said, "It wasn't?"

"No," the woman said.

We were so surprised. Janet said, "That wasn't Big Gretch."

"It wasn't?" I said.

Janet said, "No, no, that wasn't Big Gretch."

I said, "Where in the world does Big Gretch go?"

"Up and around," Buster said, "that way."

I have a terrible tale I could tell you about that. That that is.

Oh, my Mary!—I can tell you anything!

I behave myself.

I use simple words that you can understand—*the vagina of Diane, the children of Mary.* There isn't any puzzle. I could have caught sight of you I realize now.

I felt as if they were doing your fucking for you when I saw some people fucking.

Can you remember my exact words out here in the blue?

You should receive my instructions today.

I apologize, Mary, for hurting your vagina. I apologize, Mary, for being so clumsy with your vagina. My worry is, is Buster fine now? Uh, the doctor spoke to Buster. The doctor said, "Good job,

Buster."

Buster hasn't been that careful and I have had to say to Buster, "Please be careful!"

What will Buster do for me? is what I ask myself. What do you think that Buster will do for me?

Will Buster help out? Buster can be so clever. Mother is clever. It is no surprise, I suppose, that we are clever.

I spoke to Buster as frankly as I speak to you, honey.

I don't think I will ever speak so frankly again. Buster can do anything within reason with Diane and Diane agrees with me about this.

I cannot tell you how wonderful I feel when Diane tells anyone, "You are right."

Mary, I wonder what you would have done. One day you will tell me.

We have another hard week next week. It will be one thing after another.

To put it another way, it is not too difficult for us to get up into an asshole, and yet it makes some of us say our knees hurt to just think of going up there.

In driblets, we execute our duties toward Diane.

We have promised to carry her, to collect her, to distribute her, to fully dispose of her and her name. Daughter of William, second daughter of William. Born 1946. Helpful, tactful, genial—hasn't she often tried to bring herself back to the table?

Listen, she had gone off into the kitchen to get

the dessert, to bring it back to us. We were waiting for her. No one was with her in the kitchen.

We might feel a dessert is too scratched up or too cheap, that it is cheap. We could think it is thick.

Diane has to throw herself into bringing us some dessert.

"What happened to her?" we said. "Is she coming back?" Boy! She should take every opportunity to come back.

That was her in the window. We could tell by how she was hunched.

At last she peeped in.

Diane said, "Fuck me. Touch my breasts."

She comes forward. She greets you. She does not go backward. She says hello. Isn't it strange she does not go backward when we walk forward?

We make an effort to avoid getting angry with her. We try not to talk to her in a loud tone. We try not to interrupt her. We try to understand a girl when she speaks to us. We say, "Would you mind going over that again? Will you be kind enough?"

Diane doesn't have your confidence or your courage, but Mary, she is a good person.

Now Mary, Thelma is designed as my new friend.

Mr. Cohen said that I should never bring Thelma to London because they beat up people who bring Thelma to London. If she is in it, they will even burn a store to the ground in London. I can bring Thelma to Paris. Paris is fine. Mr. Cohen does not know anything about Prague. Vienna is fine.

I said I have been so careful of Thelma. I said I have never taken her anywhere. I have not fully enjoyed Thelma for all these years. I said I really wanted to take Thelma to Europe. Mr. Cohen said, "Not in the snow! because the skin cracks!"

I am aware of the risks.

I do not want people to gossip about me. You said, "I understand they question you."

We are not the only ones here.

Mary, some of us found a sexual one, but we do not have enough wisdom to take care of so many full-fledged girls and their vulvas. That we still love those girls gives us some reassurance.

A girl should be entertaining and instructive in life. Will it ever be different? Marjorie said she didn't think so.

We can celebrate in the old style. Ahead of time, we prepare.

We push our tongues, some do, into some of them, into their anuses.

"You are pretty, too!" they said.

They were the biggest, the most beautiful batch of people we have ever seen!

The eldest of our girls was the fiercest. We don't care. We hope she does come over. Something better comes along.

She was pure gold, Ma'am. We have always said she should have lived in a fairy kingdom, fitted snugly into the fairy kingdom.

It takes us so long to believe what we are saying.

Upright Pearl

How about the deity responsible for me?—why should it not move me through the realm, escort me to the other side of the predicament?

"Come now," I said, "I admire you. Can I ask you for another favor? Please, please. I am a friend of yours."

I heard singing, high and happy.

There is another oddity over the last years. I admire my darling husband. I gave him my little paw. I said to him, "Are you lonely?"

"Yes, I am," he said.

He took me by my sleeve which is wrapped in very delicate skin, so you treat it in a special way. He treats all the skin that way. We go into Illinois.

Now come the other ones who stand like peaks,

who wear the brown coat, the ochre jacket—very short.

One arrived who ate savory goldfish. She stopped. A surprise now would be best now, a nice one. The trees would not be melancholic. The lightning would be decreasing. An old woman who does not look well would show me her reliability.

The wind would roll us over a ledge and when the rain starts we would go home.

I am ashamed to say I am unhappy and we poured out liquor into our glasses and we drank it.

The disorder in my left knee has returned, and this time for a different reason than the last time, I have pallor, debilitating pain, possibly fever, a noticeable tumor involving a tendon, and persistent tingling in my affected good try and first haunting.

Ecstasy or Passion

While I am alive, I have raptures. I have troubles with my nose. When I fell, I broke both of my arms. I didn't know I had broken my arms. I sat down after I fell. There was semen on my penis. My hands were together on my belly, the way Bob's were, as if somebody had tampered with my body. Somebody else—I did not do it!—must have killed me.

Her Hair Is Red

I would not have seen the tiny indiscreet comet. I am weak. But what I think is I saw stars, stairs, stars. I have been permitted to stick these last together.

There is anything I should see.

I should stand. I comb.

Laws of nature can neglect a human. Herb helped me and my mother helped me.

I did not know she liked those grails at the house. Saw her with the sack I gave her. I should ask for a sack back for more repose of my soul.

In jam jars, she puts sundrops around and she buys small things such as toothpaste.

What I think of she provides. In fact, sure she does.

"How is Thursday," she said, "or anything else?"

There is all of this to say.

They were proud of me. There is all of that to say at the time. I was made into a more womanish girl. I tell myself not to run away, whatever that means. Thick folds of my skin prevent me, whatever that means. Rather, it is from the blather, rather, I am made.

I parade around plenty, which means I do have the globular breasts. Yet, I am watched.

Madder Lake

"Well, yes," says Jack, "but there are Frenches!"

Uh, that's very specific this time that here is Marcel French and George French and Steve. It's Steve. It's Mike. Mike's companion's name is George. He's a French. They have their obligations. That's Colleen and Marcel French and that's Sherwood French.

I'm the wriggle upright who is wearing women's slipper-type shoes.

I speak to Jack.

"In a way," I say, "I like it here." It is not difficult to understand why.

I do have the summary of quarrels. Yet, Jack and I, we are boxed in with painless prickings. We chew our morals. Our clothes are good.

Uh, that's very specific this time that it's the stuck-down Frenches—Steve and Mike French. All else is undulation and the inlaid outline.

Frenches say—"I was there." "It is my belief." "Try wide in the last four years."

Colleen French is featured with tapering legs, with a raised back. She wears her woman's head, her padded arms. I dare not to speak a word to her, in front of her, at the end of March, near her. I spoke to Jack. My feeling is I should have.

Tell Jack, Jack, tell Jack! Jack! Jack! My apron, it doesn't feel too bad. My decorated hand, my pierced-together stretcher, my displayed mount, the hanging space on every side—sliding. They do not terminate! I left lunch cooking on the stove and I made coffee!

Get myself endeared I should, endorsed with a day in mind. This day is Wednesday.

All Frenches are not dispersed. They'll lunch. A French says, "You don't usually wish?"

"Yes," Jack told Mike, "I do wish, despite my mind."

I do wish too despite my mind. I feel quite sincere and Jack is wise. I take his arm. Uh, the day—if you want one of these days I will save it for you. Jack puts his hand out for my hand, puts an arm around the waist of my madder lake crepe dress. He is one of our ablest and most crafty.

Now, for goodness' sake, here is a girl who is formal and exceedingly general.

The girl—a friend of Colleen French—says, "Are you all right? I think you're over it."

I notice the shade of the sky. This shade of sky is "orange glow," a visual effect usually created by lower skies, not often by this sort of sky which is so very high. This sort of sky's highness manages to preserve the charm of direct sunlight.

The girl says, "*Pourquoi êtes-vous si triste?*" There you are. "*Il ne faut pas être triste.*"

Our sky's so high. It's at the gravel stop of a tall building.

They Were Now at the Top

With his wife and his child he had been summoned to come forward to this moment inside of the shop.

The husband said, "Take that one."

The wife put a pair of glass frames on. She waited for her love of the glass frames to reveal itself.

The child dropped its toy. The wife began to feel hatred for her child.

"Please help me out," the wife said.

The husband said, "Take off that one."

The optician said, "Aah."

Someone else's child left the optician's shop.

"Is there a bathroom here I can use?" the wife asked.

The optician smiled. He said, "No."

Inside the bathroom a dish and a piece of soap skip like rams.

The child fell to the floor.

It spent much of its time for any reason.

"You! You ought to pick it up," the wife said to the husband, referring to the child.

"He fell!" the husband said.

"You couldn't reach it if you tried," the wife said.

D. Beech and J. Beech

Some layering is required and some combination of these people.

Maybe I did not make it refreshing enough.

Her robe has the usual fringe of snakes. She wears a wristwatch and a cheap hairclip which was a hairclip over one hundred years ago!

The whole idea is that there is the pattern. The pattern-work in the woman's head is her attitude, now worn, the upper edge of which breaks through, which meanders, which makes conversational gestures.

She could well belong to a mythological landscape against a deep pinkish orange background— or if she belongs to you—I hope you can restore her beauty.

The man or boy, he used to sit there in the morning. She would put a coverlet on him and she would pet him and she would kiss him.

Both of these people have ears which are just wrong.

It occurred during this phase yesterday that their rough tongues seemed to be merely pegged on.

It seems they live in a lush era.

He has already had his best day, the man has. The woman, she has not yet.

Now then, her hand—flat—she must do as others do.

If the two of them have really ever been tender with one another, these people, this morning, will be so mythological as if not to be yet beyond belief.

Actual People Whose Behavior
I Was Able to Observe

I want to act as if I love them and then I want to hurt at least those two during the next period of my life. For years I will do no other difficult work. I am so pleased to ruin them, you know. I said to Gor, "It will be as if they have never run around or as if they have never twisted upon their beds."

They both need affection, constant coaxing, intimacies. If I talk to them sufficiently or if somebody wiser than I am speaks to them concerning me, they will have sympathy for me, I think. I will kill you if you tell anybody I have no anal intercourse, no art treasures. I have an ideal companion I treat tactfully. I poke my hand into the air ceaselessly, as far as I am concerned.

I wipe pollen from the stamens as I was taught to

do with paper towel and put the towelling into my bowl. The water jug with the goldband lilies inside of it is like a person with a rag in her mouth. If you can believe it, the sample of cake is on a plate with a sheet of paper towelling covering it.

I said to Gor, nobody would believe it. I wear such a short skirt. I appear to be tied down by my appearance. I should look like someone I would want to see. Someone must have told me to wear this. The fur of it is like feathers. The feathers are like hair, or the feathers are hair. The fur, furry hair swishes. In the day, in the night, I am not impulsive, yet I have to urinate frequently. It was warm enough not to dress warmly. This is what is in the refrigerator. This is what is in the wardrobe—blue, black, blue, light double seams, energetic curves, slipped strokes. There is slim chance that anything is unable to be unmoved.

The Idea of Counting

It is five gems. It is eight gems. It is ten gems.
It is three gems.
It is eighteen gems.
It is five gems. It is four gems. It is five gems. It is three gems. It is three gems.
It is five gems.
It is eighteen gems!
It is three gems.
It is more than one gem.

The Duller Legend

For the duration of my speculation, the girl felt as if she had been in a world.

There is no item so common to us all as she is.

I would eat the girl's food as if it were my food. I would like to have all of her money. She has so much of it.

I try to speak the way she speaks. I wish I could wish for what she wishes for.

"Scoot the dishes off the table," said the girl. "Molly?"

The girl's urn was sobbing. The great hall—healthy and unclean—is so noisy.

The girl—though not at her worst, is not at her best—she is midway between these. A few of her live limbs flare like sprigs. Her young teeth are notorious.

A girl's guests are richly made. Unh!—a thing was perceptive.

Piercing the day is the sun with its flaws.

But that's not all. Here they have a set of sixteen greedy butter knives. Somebody is influenced by what the butter knives do.

Needing a refreshment for myself, I went into the little hills. I sought a hill, but I did not stop. In the glen, I saw three girls. My view passed from the body of one girl into the brain of another. This girl leapt toward me, yelling, dragging itself on two legs, and I went toward her, and I said, "I came looking for you to be my friend." And now I have her.

So I take this opportunity to express my deep appreciation for this most sacred object without which I do not believe my troubles would be over.

It will be interesting to see how my feelings about the girl change. In the best battle I ever fought I was supposed to meet a princess. Within days I received a handwritten letter with the warning which predicted the onslaught. She appeared in gorgeous clothing and dashed toward me, pushing ahead of the collection of pewter plates and mugs, the Turkish cooking pot, strainer and stirrer, the sparkles of hope. In the white bedroom she clung to the curve of my faith and then she sat herself down on the repetitive pattern.

A superb rider, the princess might have seen anyone or done anything. She was famous. One did not often see something so opulent. And yet, next, she threw herself round the room. Her star-studded body was famous for lavishing its attentions. We all know how hard that is if you are chunky. She is not.

That I made this last effort is not surprising. About five miles away a troop of four girls I saw was looking down into the glen. Now they are dead. They were alive. In another battle I killed five. I was married at nineteen. I have ordered my men to attack and to kill my enemies.

My career—this so-called war—one always knows how these things are going to turn out.

What else could there have been besides a battle? The baby.

The midwife had come along nicely. I heard myself say that I felt fine. A long explanation was embarked upon about flagrant kicking. No attempt was made to conceal the baby which was soon known to all as cool, intellectual, and young—the sort who moves on easily from one person to the next—is handed all around, because the thug is thoroughly emancipated.

We have banded together, the strong ones. I have engaged in sixty-five battles. Small fires are lit in the houses. The children are bathed. This is the first time I have had an infection in my mouth and it pains me to chew a juicy piece of meat. I have not been able to notice any other pain of mine.

What is this made of? I love this! See the tartan rug sits on an old chair—sits, and sits, and sits.

The Source of Authority

A sad story I heard is that I have to have someone take care of all of the bothersome aspects of my life. Tooth, leg, wrist, vein.

It feels so unsexual to complain, but when the weather is bad I go walking. I wander about, but I go to the lake because I believe the lake is better than I am and I want to be in good company. Its beauty, its success, its remote aspect, its inability to speak, hints at intelligence and virtue more pure than mine, better.

The lake means something. I rub the lake and my veins wriggle. I try to make a few things real.

There is so much silver.

Occasionally the lake looks at me coldly which gives me the creeps.

I have had no subsequent conversations with it. We speak about nothing, I tell myself.

On the shore, to myself I say, "Do you really need all of this? It's so crowded. Do you really need all this?"

I am trying to be independent. Is that wrong?

There Are So Many
Smart People Walking Around

I would be manageable if I am encouraged to eat
during these days. I should not have neglected to
eat more bread which might have been a circle with
dirt on it. This was at a grand party where loquat
pie had also been served and crayfish soup had been
served and we ate that.

When she started to eat me, I asked her if she
was tired. She said yes. I told her to sleep. Then she
cried. I brought her back to my beard to eat me. She
started to cry. I told her to sleep. She started to cry.
I asked her if she was tired. She said yes. I told her
to sleep, except that I ate her until she started to cry
again and she yelled.

Our beards thrown together caused her to yell at
me also.

You said it was ugly. It is not ugly. What if the young person is as hungry as she is tired, how can I help out? Do I keep trying to feed it, and then do I keep trying to encourage the unreasonable thing to sleep? I am only mentioning this because I thought I was supposed to. You ought to go out there and mention this question of mine as well. Mention it somewhere in an awfully nice locale I am trying to think of. I would if I were you. Is there another purpose you could go there for?

It Can Take Years to Remain

At the Fort the mister ate fat. He is made to stay inside.

He has a plan, otherwise he'll just be ill.

The missus at the foot of my chair reclines and she opens her legs so I will pet her. She is shareable. Every few hours I take her outside because it's necessary. She thinks her property will keep her from getting up in arms. If she sees her property, she thinks it keeps her from getting up into someone's arms.

At the Fort, the houses are made of Portland stone, very formal.

A steady program of repair on the heavily tree'd land leading from the Fort to the Lake is now in progress. The community has transferred the Fort to the Preservation Trust.

Several people who come through here act so bored. It's nothing surprising they prefer to emphasize the human ideal.

Ruling

This is right, more pious, they said. They leave notes in the mailbox telling me to come upstairs and they are naked. They offer me food, whatever I want. They offer me whatever I want.

In the evenings we celebrate. Other people live happily also.

I said, "I wonder if I should become beautiful again." I held the hat. I held the hat. I said, "I always want a hat, but I never wear a hat."

I put salve on my hands.

My hair is not red. My hair is yellow. My hair is brown. My hair is plaited, too. I haven't waited to walk around with a certain somebody. I said, "I like my money better than I like you. Do you need me to take care of you?"

Most said not entirely.

I put ten dollars into an envelope and I wrote on it, *For Elizabeth. Thank you. Diane Williams.* On another envelope, I wrote, *For Henry. Thank you. Diane Williams.* I put ten dollars into that envelope.

A maiden washed the twat of mine with the tan spots. The soap is red. The soap is yellow. The soap is a little bit of soap.

"How much happier do you want to be?" I was asked.

"Not much happier," I said. "A little bit happier."

I said, "Don't do that! Would you please not do that. I don't think you should do that. Are you really thinking of doing that? Is that something you would do? Have you ever done that before? I never thought you would do that. Don't do that!"

Spoon

The person has no sanction for sucking. We had surprised her while she was in the act of sucking. She was a sucker who could make a variety of noises. She was spoony—we had thought she was easy to describe. I had thought she was a wallydraigle. She might not have been. Her hair was a moderate brown and it was aimed at her head. She was suffering from vulvovaginitis.

She was too big. We had climbed into a dominion to conceive of her. She had rushed to separate the covering on her meat and on her fat. She had veins. She had turquoise eyes and her belly is a knob.

Her wan skin was her best female element.

We could have put a tumpline on her.

I have to put the worst of her into her.

A Cautionary Tale

The water is rubbed into my hair and the black hair is moistened and twirled unprettily. I hope I am not too dry for anyone.

In fact, last night in Britain, a woman came to me. We talked quite a bit about what she was—a cruel fighter. She lives in England. She has vanity, old age, ignorance, and all the rest! If I suffer, I think I please her. We drank bonnyclabber. It was this that gave— We kept talking about what we used to know, when in came another human being in a dress who dusted an inner form and the faience washstand. Did not see the babe leave, although she's all gone.

My mother said she herself would stay longer if not for my certain coolness, my unspecified dimness, my slowing down, my not-looking, my over-heard meekness in this phrase which portrays me and betrays me and portrays me and portrays me. I have fewer goings-on, even cried at times, went on lying on part of my face on the bed, fell asleep! My first few nights in sight are such rubbish. She does not want to love such a lackluster person.

The worst jolt about being loved is when it will have to start.

It Is Possible to Imagine
a More Perfect Thing

Now my father is better than my hat is. My hat is better than my mother's shoes, yet her shoes are better than these socks. My hands are better than her wristwatch. My nose is much better than her hair. My teeth are a far cry.

My carpet is inferior to her breasts, but my carpet is better than either one of my legs. My large-sized saucepot—I acted as if it is a failure compared to her personal hygiene.

I go scrub yams and put yams into the oven so that dinner can be served.

"Is this spinach?" my son said. We got a good look at it—this is clear, very active, bland, soft, runny, a fluid, a drink to drink to improve oneself with by becoming familiar with it. I acted as if I could do that.

Pricker

Everything here is bleak this, bleak that. We will see what your conclusion is. It's as if, it's as if you called to me and I did not answer you. It's as if your call to me is sufficient, but your allure is such a weakling. I am unimpressed by your allure. Or, it's as if I took my foot and squashed it inside of the squashed towel to dry it.

All over the place, after all, do you remember how I try to listen? There is a tale told about you in which you tell a better tale than this one is, one that inspires both of us—a story about something not as vague as a wet foot, veined with gray.

There it is this afternoon available from your prehistory to my present—a new reasonableness in you when you tell a person's story from various angles seen here. Really!—men love it.

Yes, true, true, you're grand to look at. You look like a nice tweed coat. You have such a kindly chirp too. We experience what is known as love, sexual intercourse, and friendship!

It is true it is difficult to talk to you in natural life conditions as a trusted friend.

What a day! Got up at 6:45. A few bashed heads. Your story is still the best story because you said you were chased by a bear, run over by a car—rather, banged into by one—and bitten by a snake. You say nothing about food even though you own a restaurant. You note the weather, what time you arrive at the restaurant, that the patio is all wet.

What a day! One is supposed to be like this and get ideas one needs!

Dear Ears, Mouth, Eyes, and Hindquarters

She crossed the main street which is enlarged by sexual stimulation. Then that's settled and I want to use the word sexy. I go for the rather goddamned bitch with my beloved arms and hands.

I have a job and I have that large now ripe sea beside us with its operation of forces.

Now she is climbing, now running, I say, trotting, typically swelling so that she can be seen. It is called profane. It is not such a time-consuming process. Imagine spending part of every day after her. She may be completely different with Mr. Reinisch who conducts her through the isolation and the cool. What is there that is good about her? Something important—this is in the land of your bitch. I had hoped to get those boners.

I want Mr. Reinisch to tell this who has the true interest to tell this.

I don't get money out of it. That is my sky and my favorable opinion of a leaf over there. That is my mother, not your mother. You would like to stop this. I would, too, but not just temporarily. You have your own mother and terraced land with vine bowers. A street runs along by many hotels, but don't bother to remember that.

It is all so multicolored. I like the stick part and what's underneath it. I just don't like the decoration on top.

I miss you!—and I want to see you! That is not such a good feeling to have at the end of the valley, at the last spur of the ridge.

Fifty Years of Quality

All the little problems of life do require solutions I need to say here, although nobody has ever come back from the north to tell me this.

"You are the only one," said Jack, "who has ever said that that hurts. You probably don't even know what your hand is supposed to feel like."

His flirtatiousness with me is not unpleasant.

I had that frothy feeling.

I saw Jack grip his hand. I thought, What did he do to his hand? Did he put his hand on the spine of a soft animal? His head and his rump were raised.

"Were you hurt?" I said, "Jack?"

He said, "No."

Together we ate a plate of almonds beforehand. I have heard the vague terms. The details of this story will become clearer—the satisfiers, the expectations, the lusters.

When I heard Jack locking doors, it is a full account of this structure because a luster can last us for fifty years.

The Description of the Worlds

I am the same as another person. There are certain circumstances I find myself in. My friends think so too. Frank or anyone does.

I have been going into another room. Coves and console brackets on the bed of the ceiling remind us many monarchs lived here.

There is not too much, fortunately, to describe. They said I found domestic life, that I eat food. I know the outcome. I am the beloved of Frank. Eventually this became a curious change Frank and I regarded highly, even if the log jumped out of the fireplace and burnt the rug in the daytime, I mean really.

Something else happened which created strong force.

I have been given the task of sweeping away my neighborhood.

I asked them to remove those little pieces of something so I could live somewhere. I like to be there, have big gardens, smaller gardens, a small unknotted garden. On Grain Street, I should ask them to remove those little pieces of something so I could live there. My description of the world is similar to Ed's. I have thought so. I know this idea I have is true, not false.

When I was asked to make a terrible mistake, I said I would not.

Bill

Of course, the ideal way to have enjoyed Bill is to have done it long ago, thoroughly. Bill was sexually mature even then. At one time Bill could be enjoyed regularly, but now sadly, no more.

Other people I know should be more like Bill. Oh, good, oh good. I can be more Bill-like than I have been. Let me tell you, don't you know I am in a position to try to understand Bill. I think he should not be wrong! Bill should be right!

I saw him!

Naturally I asked myself to remember remarks of dear Bill which seem unusual.

There are some who know what is true because they have only Bill's opinions. They settle down easily to new work, to new surroundings. These are very sensual people, extremely so!—they eat, drink, sleep.

Between ten and two I was between Bill's book-case and his table.

"Sure. Sure. Yes, well, then, good-bye," Bill said.

Before I get all upset, let me find out if Bill has really become a person who would go for a stroll.

Red Rose

Her fur neck seemed to me to be on top of her head, its color ordinary. She must have seen my neck.

Let me see what I said.

I'll have to get out, get my astonishment, and get back in here with my goggles on.

I think I do not like her genitals any more. I see hers. Under the water, it did not occur to me what she might have thought of mine. This will not be an isolated incident.

Here, again, animals, vegetables, and minerals are under or over—wedged. My body I show as a striking sword and people scold me for this.

"No! No! Don't!" she said.

She was permitted to correct me.

"If you want to, you can," I had said.

I think she should have her head and she should be authorized to wear a necklace.

My Coat

As I did before, instead of only just trying to, I tied my coat sleeves together around my waist so I was buoyed. It is less tricky not to be buoyed. I am not worried now or then, overly concerned now, troubled, bothered by my effort.

My feet are where I put them when it was too late. Bernie apologized because it was his fault. I was not supposed to show up until eleven o'clock or much earlier. I have apparently excessively walked in before I finished.

Tony

Tony's children are pretty fancy, good for everybody. These are cleverly pointy offspring I wished Tony could have because I want what's best for Tony.

They all like that word *for*.

I spent the weekend with Sally. I don't want to smooth out the edges of life by telling you how I feel about Sally.

I am not going to tell all of my enemies. I am not going to tell you—my maker, or repeatedly pester you.

May I please have a bronze flower vessel, a vase with tiger handles, edged weapons, a fine goblet and cover, a blue and white underglaze painted dish. May I please rape you?

An Inventory

She was a tree like that, a pot like that, a pan like that. I was wearing a hat like that, a wig like that.

She was becoming more earthly as I turned. I have never had any complaints about her. Do you want her?

"No," you say?

Take her, I say.

"No," you still say?

Certain other people think you must. You are making the biggest mistake of your life. She is Norwegian enough, more of an inhabitant than I thought she was. When they were holding her, she looked fatigued in the field of thought. It is an impression I have of her that is not flexible enough to be spread completely out.

I Freshly Fleshly

His block is washed clean and covered with new paper because he says one area of the block has the scent of a fish market. Because his shop window is open I have left his shop door open even wider.

Freshness and quality are just as important in people. He has a long neck and mouth, a neat fillet between foot and body, flat shoulders, and a stepped foot.

I tug on myself and cry out as if making quite an effort.

He is the only one I did that with.

"They can see us!" He leans.

"They can't see us," I say.

"They can see us!" he says.

A number of people asked him for German bologna

—an item he seldom will sell. We were rushed to the point when a woman requested half a ham. In general the customers are not too concerned. She took what she ordered and she vowed she would never return.

A man came in and after that I went home. I came home at 3:00 P.M. When I started seven years ago I was a very shy person. I don't think anyone would guess it now. The ability to meet people and to talk to anyone will be an asset all of my life. I have learned a lot about people and I have made some great friends.

Great Deed

Far off he saw his peril—that is, a friend—and she waved. So he went to her and he took her and you know it is dark. The last lantern had been put out. Have you ever?—hold this.

She intercedeth. She was lying down you know the way a woman would. Do you see what I see? She was slipping from one side to the other side. I think of her.

Finally, he said, "I can't stand this any more." He got very sick from that. He had to go to the hospital for a long time. Everybody prayed. Everybody was shaking and crying.

Every night for twenty years thereafter, stones slipped down over the rooftops and that's noisy. Finally he said, "I can't stand this any more."

Everybody was shaking. He said, "Everybody pray!" Everybody prayed. The stones stopped slipping down over rooftops. He got very sick from that. Oh, he was very sick. A lot of them had to go to the hospital. He had to go to the hospital again for a long time.

They did not have—the heat was more horrid heat than our heat. The sleep, dear guest, was sleep. Dear guest, your request not to be disturbed has been acknowledged.

Tureen

This is for me to say since the old times.

We can come in out from our history to lie down. I keep rolling their limbs between my hands, tap these gently against a hard surface, tap you against my arm, roll you lightly between my hands, break you the desired number of times. Right? Right? Right? Wrong.

On the basis of your outward appearance I may wish to vary you, to adapt you to my preferences.

You cannot be blamed, although at the end of March you spent time with my enemy.

You are not going to say any of this. Good. I am glad you are not, that I am. How long will it rain? Okay. How long will I live? Okay. Don't have any difficulties, okay?

No, I won't tell them anything about you. I won't. You don't tell them anything about me.

I am sorry I am dangerous, that I usually do and I say the wrong thing and grow old. I should not. That's what I wanted to tell you. Peter said, "It is better to make this move quickly."

Go up the stairs and you have gone quite beyond me. My room's on the first floor. This is one of the oldest human crafts—dashing on through it, being pushed through into a thing.

Wrong Hell

"Take my plate!" I said.

"No!" he said, "Not yet! Do you want these? Have you any interest in these?" he said.

They were dished up, compressed, difficult to crumble, much like any child.

"Did I do wrong?" I said.

"You did wrong," he said. "Don't cry," he said. "Don't put that there," said he. "Is it asking too much?"

"Sorry, take my plate! I am so sorry," I said.

"Don't cry," he said. "Do you want these? Have you any interest in these?" he said. The melon and the figs.

I rubbed a napkin over my hands. That is to say it's the finish of a meal even if only just a little more bleating is required. In my private act, I depend on the ending for my simpler, better, and richer act. It's not good enough, toying with figs, even if they're indispensable to enthusiasts.

"Is the salad good enough?" who says.

"Yes, yes. Ye-es. You remember? That's amazing, that last time it wasn't."

"Ye-es."

"That's remarkable that you remember."

"I remember."

"That was so long ago. She remembers!"

Tail

I would say we have a very interesting family. Ginny's husband is my cousin! We can hold her tail! My job is to inform a horde about Ginny.

I have had a hard life in my life. There is nobody else who can do what Ginny does in this country!— in the world! You could not appreciate what I say when I tell you. I can scream it from the old world when not asked to speak.

Somebody who is taller than I am or who is behind me will see Mrs. Altschuler. We thought there would be more green on her, any green on her. She is flat, covered with gold.

Understand—the best of us are not scholars or wise women. We are so-so.

The Underwear

That will be prim of you if you wear something if you have to not be home.

I tell my friends who could be similar to you—wiry arms, nipples which are not similar to mine—I am hankering to see you and I will sort of die if you do not come on over here. Hi, how are you? We need to take care of next week.

It is a trick to speak as if you would hear me. I am silken nowhere, here, by the water, by the sea, by the fleshy, thin, almost leathery bump.

The Penis Had Been Plenty Decent

The food broker, the housepainter, the swimmer and the husband's friend had liked the husband's penis very much.

The husband's penis had been plenty decent.

The wife would have walked around with the penis inside of her if that had been possible.

The husband was dead, the husband who had not been dead for very long.

The grieving wife goes to bed too late and she awakens too early and she eats a girls' party salad in the morning. She speaks about people who should receive money.

She tells people, "We have a lot to discuss."

She mourns the husband. She ties a mortifying scarf around her waist which had been the husband's own. She wears his unmerciful nightshirt. She wears the frown which had once belonged to her husband's mother.

Then she clumsily prepares a miracle.

The Brilliants

The sky might not have been too disorganized for them. The clouds were innately ornate. There were too many clouds.

The man was elated by the abundance of decorative clouds, by their prominence.

The man picked up off of the ground scraps of anything from trees. On that particular day, the woman had forgotten her purpose.

Yet on another day, the woman had been the one to clean up. She vacuumed. She washed. She sponged the surface of a bottle of mineral water. She rinsed the nail parings down the drain. The sink was wetted with greasy water, leftover water, yellow water, white watery water, water which is not transparent water. This is water.

The water has only been appreciated since the beginning of last week, after the discovery of the patches of iridescence in it.

The water is somewhat rare, has a slight turbidity. The value of water is fairly low, has a very low value, the lowest.

The woman and the man are of modest value.

One method is used to determine their value—mine.

Pairs of people have a relatively unimportant vitreous luster. They command sympathy, have heart attacks, weeping spells. They grow suspicious.

A man alone in the natural world is tidy.

Yellower

The house looks younger and yellower and yellower. The dog appears larger and proud. The house is much skinnier.

The dweller looked smaller and humble and smaller. Her husband looks fatter.

Everything is fine, but not much greener. On Friday her husband will do anything if its characteristics are not insisted upon.

Large Organization

Malus held a dog who tongued her hand as Caladium told her what she should not do. If she did that, Caladium said, he would not think she was a special person any more.

The dog wore a condom.

"That is not to say," Caladium had said, "that every time you give a tour it's a poor idea, or that your tours are harmful. I am saying that when you think, Let me give a tour, let me introduce myself so I can talk to you—don't do that. Don't. It would be better for you if someone came up from behind you and pushed you into an automobile or truth."

They didn't like my listening—so I walked along the sweep and I heard a boom crane.

In the sweep, another dog grew bold. This dog

played beautifully with a boy.

The dog dragged down its haunches and produced an object about the same size and shape as the boy's phallus.

Now I can understand the difference between "systems." I can understand the normal sequence of events—even simplified information I can understand, and which hairstyle I get. The question always becomes for me—who becomes my friend?

Cake

I am four feet long. I am no bigger than a dust mop. I won't bite you. That is something Tom would say. Tom would want to blurt it out.

When I got here, I said to myself, "I hope he's here."

He fed me cake which is particularly bulky, medium to large, covered with rigmarole, quality good, pleasant, striped with carmine.

He is medium, pleasant.

He cleans stains from the two quart aluminum saucepan. He does not show undue concern.

He is as beautifully browned as the beautiful girls in fancy bakeries.

So many times he was heard to say, "I wouldn't mind being here if I only knew I was supposed to."

I am comfortable at a table or desk, eating.

The table is by the window. This is not a nightmare view of life.

I was filled up. I was bubbling one day. I am changing. I am changing. I am different!

I want to gratify my little cock, but I do not want to be thick. I do not want to thicken up the way Diane Williams did. I talked to her. She said the services are not as good. Well, she said, they are still as good, but you have to ask for them. It used to be you didn't have to ask.

Actually, he stood by me while I was bathed. The flattened hollow of my back is where there is a spot to brush the edge of.

I eat cheese on toast most mornings. What would Diane Williams think about me? What?

I'll find out all about it at dinner and then I may change my mind about my life.

What a triumph to have food placed before me for me, so long as you and I meet.

Arm

My favorites among my limbs and my many patches of skin—anything he asks for that belongs to him—I want to keep those. A nice bright unsealed box of his he did not, in fact, give me, I want.

I could not relieve myself of an entire region, please! I want to keep those.

There is a nice naturalness of his I'll keep. His seriousness of purpose which he advances, I want.

I am so tired, though, of a nice bright sensation. Back it goes to him!

My patience is his.

Row of Us Surrounded by
Seven Slightly Smaller Ones

Her future will have been brought to a sad end if it is not incessantly, daily decorated.

The Williams woman opened the gift from me. The immoral wrapping paper lay on her leg.

"Oh, please and thank you!" she said.

"You are loved," I say. "Would you like to play a game of checkers or of chess?"

"Oh! I am very tired. I am just too tired. I am waiting for my boys and then I am going upstairs."

She wears several small jewels and lesser chains, a waist buckle, shoe buckles, and an arrow brooch.

When a big jewel was handed over to the woman, I said, "Do you really like it? Do you really like it? No, I really mean it. Do you really like it? Tell me how much you like it."

She said, "I cannot remember."

So said, so seen. I will tell you I was an elder clothed and fed.

I would like to go to that store to get gemstones for her to wear with that gemstone, something with a crystal! When was the last time I knew what was best for someone?

Most nights I never knew if I was going to give her a thrum or a finger ring. Tonight she gets a particle of something.

A Woman's Fate

This suggests that exposure to her may have been difficult, that an animal became sluggish instantly in her vicinity and dragged its tail along the paving. I am terribly sorry because this was a creature destined for a habit of vigorous walking, who is restrained from too much activity. I do not want to make a joke of this. Every animal I know is extremely sad or a little sad.

On her fence sat an animal with its face turned away from her. Its penis was at an upturn, and she called authorities to inquire about that one. There is something in her inquiry which is a shriek.

In swollen volume, animals dawdle beneath her auto and they surround her auto. She notifies authorities. Come here. I want you to feel what this is like.

An animal on her roof—its silhouette revealing a narrow waist—spit—spat its acorn at her.

Certain animals have intentions to awe, to comfort, to guide, to be gossipy—to be observant, to be sly, to be thoughtful, and more. To be witty, to come to light, to be worth waiting for.

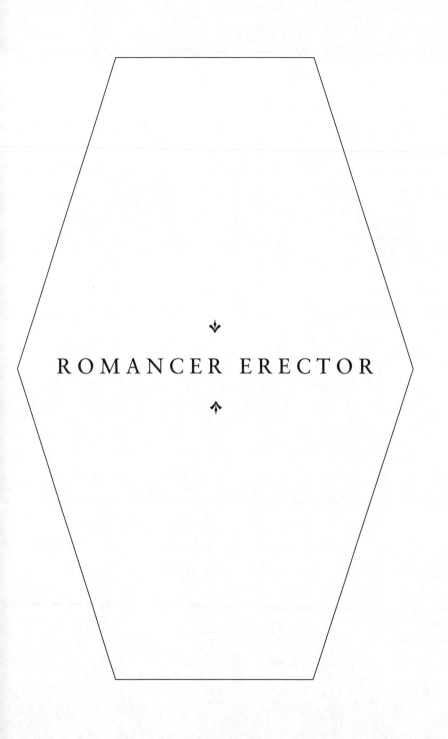

ROMANCER ERECTOR

1

How keen I have been with my thinning mind, with my large feet in new shoes, to have this life story. I feel unsteady and am afraid of my boyfriend. I unbutton my vest. I say, "Isn't he marvelous, an adorable boy!"

The boy gives me a piece of cheese rind and a bit of paper and a gherkin on a plate. His clothing is stained. I admire him. He touches my breast.

For now, there's a slight bulge in my acumen.

Soon I laugh and am willing to stay the night. When asked I say, "I will."

Before my old eyes there is old pottery and a gilt chair, and an unold mouth about to kiss me.

I'll wind up in this position with the boy's father, our host, Don Musgrave.

I regard the boy's boyishness in the morning. How short he is and very serious. He sits at a desk drawing on paper with crayon. Other children fight in the room next to us.

I show part of my breast and he puts crayon marks on paper. I dress myself and tease him.

"Can I have a drink of water?" the boy says.

Whenever he does not speak to me, something mysterious and significant will happen. Already there has been my crawling around in a bed stretching out his penis in the hope I can find lasting companionship.

The child says not much more but is aggressive as if in romantic trouble.

A grand dark pink river is visible beyond the window. This is the dark pink River Urine.

You'll see. Oh, it's all very well.

As a woman of my own devising I have had an actual undoing—a fairly smooth, horizontal, waist-high undoing—at this residence.

I took the bedding downstairs for washing.

It was streaming, shaking, teetering. I like the bed.

If it isn't peaceful here, it isn't because of the cooked supper, the baths, the whiskey, and all of the ginger ale.

Mrs. Musgrave turns on the light switch. She goes to the boy whose face is lined and fair. There is gray in the child's hair and the child digs a hole in his mother or something. Then the mother groans. The

child's charm briefly appears. Two other guests—
the Burgundys—keep speaking coarsely.

The boy is taken upstairs and Mrs. Burgundy gets
a towel.

I caress the back of my unwarm neck. The enor-
mousness of my love for someone makes me sud-
denly drowsy.

The dirty Burgundys are the first guests to go
home.

I'd be willing just to take a nap.

I move as if I do some sort of work—a jerky sort
of rocking while seated, not for long.

I choose a place to sit between their boy—their
son—and an older man.

I suppose we all undulate to the music of my
father.

The penis of the boy comes to mind and flour-
ishes gaily.

This river water is stiffer than river water should
be, not a good red, but a poor pink color.

I make for myself a light or dark brown flowing
cup of coffee.

That Musgrave boy with gray, black-tipped hair
is now bathing. Yeah, I hear that a lot—that this
has nothing to do with sexuality or experts or alli-
ances or innovating or proliferating. Yeah, I hear
that a lot.

A tiny piece of paper with tape is on the table. I
give up. Oh, stop it. I pick up the piece of paper.

What does it say on it? I rub the paper between my fingers. Two more boys in the house are short.

Mrs. Musgrave has fed the boys and she sits down against a tree. We'll have fried pies, then see some photographs. I hope Don gets an erection.

I know myself as a small person with light brown skin. I am bald and I wear a substantial wig. I have brown eyes and a pathetically narrow skull and am in the same room with men and people I have not adequately described.

I'm in the gala room, having passed beneath the carved swag to the entrance door. I have to go to the bathroom.

I'll produce a dribble of cruelty, that's all. The only fine chair fills in a gap.

The rock-crystal chandelier is lit.

I stumble on the drugget enroute to the bathroom.

I don't know what the reason is people don't wear their hats, such a marked drop in the hats.

The storm, the feast, the fear, a big romance—yes—that's what I want. I don't want to be rude, but I have to stop speaking to you. I have to go to the bathroom.

The next day several men mention to me how thin the boy is. He really looks very thin. I thought it could be the strain of all this. He, the boy, just begs me to sit at the table. There really isn't room. Marge sets the soup bowl down in front of me. Very well. The boy has his head on his hands. I drink soup this morning. Am not feeling well. The boy invited two of his friends over, actually he invited three. There are three new young boys here, very nice young boys, very nice. I really appreciate boys, as I say.

So, what I am saying is I know where to go from here.

All across the bourne, even in the village, going past the vegetable store, I feel fear now. The fear is so conjunctive to my life.

I see Musgrave, the tall man. His hair is black and white. His skin is dark and light.

True, the boy is here this evening again not speaking to me. He isn't looking for me. He isn't in love with me, or wishing for me, or is he all of that? We had fun. I have fun. What we had was fun. I hardly ever have fun.

Musgrave went to the drawing room. He picked up an apple from a bowl. He must have heard the boy, his son, cry out. Musgrave may have thought this signalled the complete change of the world. I do not.

My shoes are made of kidskin with a silk ruche at the front. I wear a dress with an unusual striped working of the fabric.

There may be a similarity between Don Musgrave and me—a slight fullness of the throat, deep creases about the cheeks. I am unique, exclusive and have a desire today not to be disgusted by my excrement.

Forgot to mention the dogs are abounding as are all the animals clinging to the land and the air— hanging onto each other and getting ready to go.

Do you do any more with this? This encampment is on the River, on the corner diagonally across from the other corner on which stands the Church of Transfiguration. The encampment is very small and is slightly under the overlapping folds of its surroundings. It narrows into an almond shape with a frowning expression and is sometimes cranky. Not surprisingly, I want to give it pleasure.

2

It's as if the Musgraves work harder than I do.

They talk to me. They give me money. I don't have much money. I remove my soiled wig.

Nobody ever asks me to explain myself.

They tell me to keep myself as clean as a guest, to put on clean clothes. I get my pullover sweater.

It's as if I have said, "Give me one of your sons." Their son gives me a hand carrying parcels.

So what if I am afraid. I love to be with young kids. His eyelid area is rounded. His lower lids swell. He has a triangular face, fleshy hands. Everybody loves this boy.

One night his dad told me to sit down or to lie down on the mat.

"What is it?" I say. I say, "Tell me what's wrong."

His dad's a little upset. Yes, I can imagine. The fact is—well—the walls are papered in sheets of gold. The ceiling was painted by Michel Corneille.

Musgrave is tasteful and urgent. His is a famous form. He isn't lucky with his wife. I come here all the time and he gives me clothes. I'm at it—I want to have a big romance.

"What is it?" I say. I say, "Tell me what's wrong."

"What I thought was wrong with you," he says, "is the same thing that is wrong with everyone else."

This is a fine important courtship.

This is for me a time of great ease and I do not know now if it will last and last and if this will be the end of my old, impure world.

He says, "Harder, even harder." He pulls up my clothes. He's American. The rubbing he does is on my front beneath the hair.

"You don't have to do that unless it gets you excited," he says. "I'm going to the bathroom."

I loll while he uses the facilities. Yeah, I've been running around all weekend, sort of like a crazed man.

As if I am a man, I take my leave. Sometimes it's a good thing to let someone know what's up—hurrying away, on my lark, unruly-like at the rim of Olive Woods. Shoppers like me often appear, sidling around buildings, far from the river.

I was born in this city near the River Urine on the western shore of it.

Bought a replacement fluorescent tube bulb for the kitchen. At the hardware store the proprietor Jen says she suffers from a glandular deficiency.

Better if I am dignified, trying to walk back to the house into this valley. There's the faint sight of the fright in the sky.

I remind you I wear a wig plus the unguent. I have small breasts and a sharp-edged collarbone and hard flesh. My nose is long and my eyes are slits.

It is difficult to explain the true details of my head. I am two-thirds life-size.

My costume ties behind my neck and fits gracefully over my trousers. I have chains and strings of rubies and corals around my neck.

Back at the residence I am a guest again with the rest, on the lawn, in my gown eating a sandwich and drinking apple juice. My fingernails are yellow and outlined in red stain.

At the top of the sky is the sun, but it is not in its usual place. A house servant delivers another aristocratic dish of food which she says we'll like. I think everybody is very warm and nice. That is so sweet and I am very surprised. Yeah, that is really, really sweet.

We eat large pieces of food. All the salad ingredients have been cut into cubes from which any excess taste has been drained off. A pie is served, but is so carelessly guarded that it is eaten.

I re-bandage my finger, kiss the dog on its chin.

A vase of tomato-red, slow-walking tulips is on a table.

I gather I am bell-shaped and am fond of this shape. My ensemble has a sash, is printed in a shade of turquoise. I wear a beautiful ring which is really carat gold.

The Musgrave boy brings himself crookedly backward, farther away from me. I do not pity him. He'll be happy or unhappy. I tell him a story and swipe the top of his head.

The boy goes to sit with other boys who are hardly seen and that is why they are hardly formed.

Some additional female figures come out onto the lawn—young women and an old woman. The old woman carries two juice jars.

I would like to thank Penny Gorell for all her help. I insist on giving her a kiss.

Our hostess thinks it is time for you to go.

3

If we start again there is a vase of peonies respectably standing.

I see the sofa I am sodomized on often enough. I remind you I wear a black wig and have embellishing ointments on my neck, face, arms, and legs.

Although I qualify for a big romance, most nights I am in bed by myself because the child who could be at my side has strep throat.

Let me start again to be sweeter. I will cook Gooseberry Fool for a meal.

Flat on their backs, folks have their hips off the floor a few inches. Dirty, glamorous, haggard ones work the muscles around their rectums so they may propagate.

Cora—Cora Musgrave—she's the mother—says

she'll cook the cutlets.

She has slanting eyes, a ruler's face. The Musgrave group is slender, although Cora has her pendulous breasts.

I like to think my pubic area is fresh with a round edge. Mightn't everything of mine be so excellent?

A few times to depict humans, I describe our faces.

"Why don't you let me do that?" Cora says, as she beats the egg whites well.

When I see her boy next, I think of him as a good hurry-up—ritzy and crunchy and pleasing and outstanding and I appreciate how mercy is embedded in this furnished room.

For an example of soothing ornaments, see the view of the bathroom which shows off the toilet and a sink, you know, and the trash basket.

4

I think Cora's concerned for me because she's next to me and she's large. When I dab at her in private, in theory, I get excited.

She puts the Fool—with its fluffed, lively flavor—it's really delish—on a tile.

We have Skillet Toast John Bixby, the cutlets as well, and coolers, and milk drinks, and types of tea.

Cora suggests that I need to rush off.

The point is I head for the Midwest in a Boeing Triple 7 and my abdomen seems enlarged. I see the crisscross of the shiny brown church and several better-perceived burnt sienna clouds that we abandon over The Variety Store.

The River exhibits its shortness of breath but must have a somewhat normal urinary flow. Come now,

I could congratulate myself and be politely interested in all.

I travel with my ordinary empty female tube. I prefer to visit universities and I like a high value life and why can't I be in good spirits?

To scrutinize a few routine matters, I pay a visit to my office.

5

To two medium pieces of bread I add a pulpy center and with it drink a grapefuit Brazilian cocktail I find in the office fridge.

The process of letting my spirit rise in a warm place until it's double its size used to occur more often than it does now as I sit at my desk.

I make notes, study my work schedule, drink up, forgo indifference. I take a brief nap in my chair. I awake at 4:00 P.M. to interview a staff member concerning a project she works on.

I have to have this exchange with her—that I will fondle someone but that I will not be fondling her.

She causes herself to crouch. Some saliva of hers becomes explosive, as if she's being flattened under the pressure of being squelched.

A little later I slither back in a DC-10 to my Musgrave life. In the rear of the house are tiny rooms. There's a wide carpeted staircase leading upstairs— a somewhat vivid elegance is suggested by sofas, paintings, and good crystal chandeliers. Nothing is so merry, so hopeful as rooms in which there are garlands, bow-knots, quivers, and a great deal of plaster panelling. Right?

Here beauty does not depend on repairs being made as soon as is possible.

My neck doesn't look that good any more and Don says that's because that's where people have tried to strangle me.

6

It took me several hours to assess my point of view and to decide I am a slut. The excitement produced by this point of view affords a clue to its usefulness. People have had some tussles and some arguments with me.

I go out to The River, take along my umbrella.

I feel sorry for anyone who doesn't feel as I do. Feel terribly sorry. I turn around to regard some of the forces of life. There is another one of them every time I turn around. The orchard within my reach has a complex past and the trees are fragile and servile.

Toward the end of the day I am angry. You won't have to know much about it. If only I'd say one thing which is of interest to you as if I authentically love either you or the little boy.

I'm damned if Cora didn't yell that dinner is ready.

She has been put into a dinner gown woven with silver and gold scrolls and I wear a beaded bolero. The Duke is in a dinner suit of navy tabby-weave suiting. He prefers American-style trousers. I am, I gather, in a tight-fitting Mexican costume with a self-tie belt.

Bare-skulled, I wear no wristwatch and wonder if I ought to put down my whisky. I get up because I am achy. One leg is.

If you're here, you'll have some things and the food which is good later. Whole wheat bread!—no-meat croquettes, and creamed green beans!

The beginning of the world feeling ought to be exhilarating. The eager breeze outside looks to have blood in it.

It might just have easily given me the cold shoulder. I say this storm's deeply attracted to me. I grant that that's unlikely. I just get a gander through the window so it can throw itself into me body and soul. Its every sound—gentle and old hat—I've not heard all of them before. This strong, very handsome storm sure likes to take me down.

Don Musgrave, though—he has given me so many gifts—coins and a gold ring. He stands to give me more with his left foot forward, arms bent at the elbows. His tunic is hiked and his genitals are exposed. My elaborately curled wig is back on, so I am confident and I am confident I have gotten the most money from him by taking his contributions.

His scalp is covered with fine black hair. He has clipped his fingernails recently. He has a newborn baby's eyes, almost as cross-eyed as mine.

Since his sex organs have become so apparent, I touch the top of them. He passes himself to me, under my gown, internally and so forth, and when my bladder's neck is unavoidably compressed, I feel desire.

I begin to think I should think this is a feeling of happiness.

The reasons are several-fold. In the first place Mr. Musgrave exerts pressure on my upper abdomen. In the second place, I have fallen hard against my side where the zipper on my side is kind-hearted and wobbly.

Upon arising I drink a glass or two of cold water and have moderate vaginal discharge.

7

The real story begins on Thursday—pungent, warming—the translucent tale.

My umbrella with its bulbous base is being rolled, closed, and snapped. It and I are twining on the untroubled, dampened lane.

The River is carmine today, or say scarlet, or say The River has bled, you say.

It is a day later and I begin the sudden act. I look at the body of the house, at its creamy broad tail. I go through the business of staying here again. I lift myself up out from under my droop, up and out from under my prevailing tone. When I appear inside the house, Cora says, "Please, please."

I go over to her and slam my palm against the back of her arm. How that may have hurt her.

Please, people like me should just step back. I say, "All right. It's your house!"

Her Jewish face is damp. What else is there I could call her face?

The dog has its tongue on the cat's tongue.

I find my head aches, it's itchy and my wig is a big bother. I take up my hand, try that again—I push her, but Cora does not fall. I pull her arm, we fall. I sit, not unlike a beast.

"Dear," I say, "get up." I say, "All right."

She leaves the room, you understand.

On both sides of me are bright little things—the silver ewer and basin, a pair of candlesticks that are wildly popular. But you know perfectly well no one has fainted or is dead yet.

I have storyish ideas but no story in me. This is the row of empty marks. These are the signs of what is next.

Don't I listen? We could get someone else to talk to me. Here is—well, well, here is—is it really one of you?

8

You would know what I know about your facets. However, it's exciting if I tell you something which gives you a better understanding of your androgynous nature, your natural furrows.

The holes for your eyes are filled, but what do you think?

The upper lip of your mouth is double arched. There is enough of your neck to show your neck muscles. Your clothing is partly open.

Admittedly, you speak and I cannot hear it.

Do you think, Why so much stuff on their sideboard? You don't, do you, want to be with a woman who can have so much more of anything than you can have?

This is my friend Kim Burgundy, my friends Steve,

Cora, and Don.

Should we change the furnishings?—the textiles and the relics are nice. Nice enough for you?

I hear, "How could you do this? This is so cruel!"

Now I am tired of drama. The nation, the American people want it to be over. Thought you'd want to have a nice supper, kiss me and never let me go. As far as I know you just got here. Ever since the storm, the house has had a wide opening with no door on it.

I know you got in, that you've been here, but not really in the saloon or in the boudoir.

When I was young, I used to see the worst in everyone. You look slightly confused. If there's one thing I can't stand it's a puzzle in the mind or a bad crack in an argument. Surprisingly Steve Burgundy— are you aware?—is eyeing you, owing perhaps to your charms.

My acquaintances are pretty much as you might expect—propping themselves up with their pals inside of some unimportant closet or passageway. At the first sign—if you feel an examining hand proceeding smoothly—even that old bugbear pain or what could constitute murder could, of course, happen here however nonchalant I may behave during a disturbance.

"I will take you myself," Steve says.

"Where to ?" I say. "To where will you take our guest?"

9

So, um, what do I think our next step might be? There's no protocol here to be quiet. Steve seems somewhat insubstantial, as do you. You can still have a cup of coffee or something, a melon slice, a cup of punch.

You might as well have a public possibility on the settee, in a bed, in the grove.

You will have to produce at least flecks of rugged individualism. This is America!

Begin to tiptoe into some of these areas with your practical, your personal concerns.

This may seem unreasonable to you or out of the blue, crude. You can go to bed, have coffee—aspirin and honey. Anything you like.

We'll find out if Steve is flimsy, or is he living a

normal life again? He's got his hands in the pockets of his dressing gown. I had forgotten how harsh his voice can be. It will take too great an effort to have him do or say anything more.

10

There's a great golden gob of curtain that's as fucked up as something else I can think of—oh, so lovingly. The velvet curtains in the saloon are drawn, yet not completely closed.

I am not halfway up the stairs when I hear the nearly unimaginable boy call my name. Oh, fucking!—after all, there is time for it.

The bedroom's brightened by wax candles which show off gimcracks.

The child tries to harden himself and I am pretty well done some time after midnight.

Before breakfast he's got some pleasant news to give me.

11

This is worth one thousand dollars that the boy is—first of all, there'll be no more worrying what he will like or not like.

Any more explaining the truth—you'd have to be the one to tell me.

There is grease on the floor, my areola are puffy. This alliance is worry free.

There's a moment of agitation. I know it is the last moment of agitation, the beginning of a new sinful moment. Therewith I say, to be sort of dreadful, "I want you to see if you can clean up your room." He suggests I drive the car which I will not do to buy him a toy.

Trusting that more moments will occur from day to day—that muscular cramps occur, it most certainly is not my intention to suggest more sexing now.

12

Mrs. Donald Musgrave may just feel she should toil some more. She puts her good arm up in the air and then lets it fall down. She faces the bread crumbs.

I remind myself I am a guest, am not at my own home. I do not congratulate myself, but I go out onto the lawn.

A richly carved tree trunk is situated by a slope, by the discarded past. The River when it's seen is a cut gush.

Thought maybe I should have dressed for work. The way I stay—as if I am a man, as if I stand up and first shove my erection into my trousers with my ungloved hand—I stay here hurrying.

What a day. Even away from the office—standard stuff—bookwork must be done. I need to make adjustments of smaller losses. My employer, like any other, wants as much speed and accuracy as possible.

This visit to the householders takes up a lot of my time.

13

A group is yapping away.

Put back your head.

It is very offensive, all unkind words.

Yet life is often good in this district behind homely facades. This is a town that may give up. I love how it's built on no one annoying thing, on nothing even resembling that, that might not have sentimental value.

14

I guess I care more for carnal love, more than I care for Cora Musgrave or for her domain.

Not surprisingly the sexual congress with little Musgrave is excusable conduct. We're just plain people with our hands on each other.

What I must be prepared to do—my job spills over into my leisure hours—my particular hopes and frustrations.

I wouldn't mind knowing better how to fix things and how to feed a family well.

If there is any great American meal it might be braised beef balls and creamed potatoes, or say lamb shanks with pepper gravy, or lamb shoulder chops with crispy crackers and butter, right?

In effect, what relation is there between a person's

work life and home life?

Volumes have been written about what every person should know.

15

Ho!

What sort of blood and mushroom dish is this they serve?

The host drinks a Side Car and his wife, you know, (whose body is well-marked by violet veins) wears a good orange jewel.

My discussions—I have heard them described— my costume, my string of beads. My boudoir in the guest wing forms the backbone.

16

For the good of the country, men come down the stairs.

Don Musgrave loses his balance and he falls, then stands which is not difficult for him to do if he keeps his knees bent and his feet flat.

My arms—my hair is in outright fleshy strands! The natural distance between my breasts is rather too slim to receive the slab of his outstretched hand.

17

"You're not getting any more money," Don tells me.

At present I am thinking one thousand or two.

If it needs to be different, this is the end. Hmm, before bed, I take a Centrum Performance. I put the child at the end, at the end of the bed and I do think people should stop their work for family or for the social visit of a friend.

Okay, okay, okay, okay, okay, okay, okay.

SELECTED DALKEY ARCHIVE PAPERBACKS

Pierre Albert-Birot, *Grabinoulor*.
Yuz Aleshkovsky, *Kangaroo*.
Felipe Alfau, *Chromos*.
   Locos.
   Sentimental Songs.
Alan Ansen, *Contact Highs: Selected Poems 1957-1987*.
David Antin, *Talking*.
Djuna Barnes, *Ladies Almanack*.
   Ryder.
John Barth, *LETTERS*.
   Sabbatical.
Augusto Roa Bastos, *I the Supreme*.
Andrei Bitov, *Pushkin House*.
Roger Boylan, *Killoyle*.
Christine Brooke-Rose, *Amalgamemnon*.
Gerald L. Bruns,
   Modern Poetry and the Idea of Language.
Gabrielle Burton, *Heartbreak Hotel*.
Michel Butor,
   Portrait of the Artist as a Young Ape.
Julieta Campos, *The Fear of Losing Eurydice*.
Anne Carson, *Eros the Bittersweet*.
Camilo José Cela, *The Hive*.
Louis-Ferdinand Céline, *Castle to Castle*.
   London Bridge.
   North.
   Rigadoon.
Hugo Charteris, *The Tide Is Right*.
Jerome Charyn, *The Tar Baby*.
Marc Cholodenko, *Mordechai Schamz*.
Emily Holmes Coleman, *The Shutter of Snow*.
Robert Coover, *A Night at the Movies*.
Stanley Crawford, *Some Instructions to My Wife*.
Robert Creeley, *Collected Prose*.
René Crevel, *Putting My Foot in It*.
Ralph Cusack, *Cadenza*.
Susan Daitch, *Storytown*.
Peter Dimock,
   A Short Rhetoric for Leaving the Family.
Coleman Dowell, *The Houses of Children*.
   Island People.
   Too Much Flesh and Jabez.
Rikki Ducornet, *The Complete Butcher's Tales*.
   The Fountains of Neptune.
   The Jade Cabinet.
   Phosphor in Dreamland.
   The Stain.
William Eastlake, *The Bamboo Bed*.
   Castle Keep.
   Lyric of the Circle Heart.
Stanley Elkin, *Boswell: A Modern Comedy*.
   Criers and Kibitzers, Kibitzers and Criers.
   The Dick Gibson Show.
   The Franchiser.
   The MacGuffin.
   The Magic Kingdom.
   The Rabbi of Lud.
Annie Ernaux, *Cleaned Out*.
Lauren Fairbanks, *Muzzle Thyself*.
   Sister Carrie.
Leslie A. Fiedler,
   Love and Death in the American Novel.
Ford Madox Ford, *The March of Literature*.
Janice Galloway, *Foreign Parts*.
   The Trick Is to Keep Breathing.
William H. Gass, *The Tunnel*.
   Willie Masters' Lonesome Wife.
Etienne Gilson, *The Arts of the Beautiful*.
   Forms and Substances in the Arts.
C. S. Giscombe, *Giscome Road*.
   Here.
Karen Elizabeth Gordon, *The Red Shoes*.
Patrick Grainville, *The Cave of Heaven*.
Henry Green, *Blindness*.
   Concluding.
   Doting.
   Nothing.
Jiří Gruša, *The Questionnaire*.
John Hawkes, *Whistlejacket*.
Aldous Huxley, *Antic Hay*.
   Crome Yellow.
   Point Counter Point.
   Those Barren Leaves.
   Time Must Have a Stop.
Gert Jonke, *Geometric Regional Novel*.
Danilo Kiš, *A Tomb for Boris Davidovich*.
Tadeusz Konwicki, *A Minor Apocalypse*.
   The Polish Complex.
Elaine Kraf, *The Princess of 72nd Street*.
Ewa Kuryluk, *Century 21*.
Deborah Levy, *Billy and Girl*.
José Lezama Lima, *Paradiso*.
Osman Lins, *The Queen of the Prisons of Greece*.
Alf Mac Lochlainn, *The Corpus in the Library*.
   Out of Focus.
D. Keith Mano, *Take Five*.
Ben Marcus, *The Age of Wire and String*.
Wallace Markfield, *Teitlebaum's Window*.
   To an Early Grave.
David Markson, *Reader's Block*.
   Springer's Progress.
   Wittgenstein's Mistress.
Carole Maso, *AVA*.
Harry Mathews, *Cigarettes*.
   The Conversions.
   The Journalist.

FOR A FULL LIST OF PUBLICATIONS, VISIT:
www.dalkeyarchive.com

SELECTED DALKEY ARCHIVE PAPERBACKS

FOR A FULL LIST OF PUBLICATIONS, VISIT:
www.dalkeyarchive.com